Walt Disney's

Lady and *the* *Tramp*

Based on Walt Disney Company's
full-length animated feature film

This adaptation by
Victoria Crenson

TROLL ASSOCIATES

Chapter One

An air of excitement hung over the town, for it was Christmas Eve afternoon. Giant snowflakes drifted down. Shoppers trudged through the snow carrying gaily wrapped presents and bunches of holly.

Among the crowd, Darling and Jim, a young couple who had married the past summer, were holding hands and laughing as they tried to keep their balance on the slippery ground. A snowflake landed on the tip of Darling's nose. She brushed it away, then said, "Oh, Jim dear, there's a pet shop! I want to look in the window."

"Come on then," replied Jim with a laugh.

Darling pressed her nose against the glass. "Oooohh...just look at that adorable little puppy! Isn't she the sweetest thing you ever saw?"

"Which one?" replied Jim Dear.

"The little golden spaniel, of course. She's looking right at us. What gorgeous eyes she has."

"Yes, she is pretty, but come on, Darling. We have to go home and decorate the tree."

Reluctantly, Darling turned away from the pet shop window, the pup's eyes following her. Darling turned to get a last glimpse of the tiny spaniel before joining Jim Dear and heading for home.

Later at home, while Darling was adding the final touches to the Christmas tree, Jim Dear slipped softly out of the house. Darling did not see him go. She was busy arranging tinsel on the tree's branches. "Oops..I almost forgot to put Jim dear's presents under the tree," she said aloud. "I wonder where he is." She had just placed them under the tree when the livingroom door opened and Jim Dear came in.

"The tree looks lovely," he said. "Darling, please go into the other room a minute and promise not to peek."

"It sounds mysterious...but very exciting," laughed Darling, walking into the kitchen.

A few minutes later Jim Dear called her. "Your presents are under the tree, Darling, but tonight you can open just one."

"Which one shall I open?" said Darling looking at the assortment of packages.

"That one," smiled Jim Dear, pointing to a hat box tied up with red ribbon. Bending over, he picked it up and handed it to her.

"Wow!" said Darling. "One thing is for certain. It can't be a hat. Its much too heavy. Its sagging at the bottom." She placed it on the floor and untied the ribbons.

Suddenly the lid rose up and a pair of big brown eyes peeped up at her.

"A present especially for you, Darling. A very merry Christmas." Jim Dear watched his wife, a happy grin on his face.

"Oh..oh, Jim dear, I can hardly believe it! What a wonderful gift." Darling reached in the box and lifted out the tiny golden spaniel puppy wearing a cute pink ribbon.

Raising the puppy to her face she gazed into its eyes. The pup put out her tongue and lovingly licked Darling's cheek. "She's saying hello," laughed Darling.
Jim Dear gently stroked the puppy's fur. "You like her, Darling?"

"I love her. What a perfectly beautiful little lady. That's what I'll call her. Lady!"

The tiny pup had found a good mistress and a good home. For her that was the best Christmas present!

Chapter Two

Almost six months had passed since the Christmas Eve when Lady had first entered Jim Dear and Darling's life. She was a member of the family. Life was good and she was happy. She loved her master and mistress with true doggie devotion.

It was six o'clock on a beautiful summer morning when Lady awoke. She licked Darling's sleeping face, then jumped down to the floor. Yes...it was a great day and time to be up. Running around the foot of the bed, she licked Jim Dear's hand as it hung outside the covers. He didn't move so she put her wet pink nose under the sheet until she found his toe and tugged gently at it until Jim Dear woke up.

He sat up with a start. "It's all right,

Lady. Take it easy girl, I'm awake. What time is it? I'm getting up... okay...I'm up." Jim stumbled unsteadily to his feet. He glanced at the clock.

"Oh dear, Lady...you've done it again."

"Done what again?" Darling's voice was a sleepy question.

Jim Dear staggered back to bed, pulling the covers up around his ears. "Can't you explain to Lady about Sundays? She insists that I go to work seven days a week," he yawned.

Lady scampered around the bed to her mistress. "Go on, girl, go out in the garden and play," said Darling. She watched Lady scamper towards the bedroom door, then she, too, snuggled back under the covers.

Lady bounded down the stairs and through her private swinging door into the garden. With a loud happy bark, Lady chased the birds away and trotted over to a bone she had tucked away the evening before. She dragged it over to a tulip bed and busily dug a hole to bury it in. Dirt flew in all directions. So did a tulip. Lady knew that Jim Dear would be annoyed. So Lady replanted the tulip and merrily bounded away, not knowing she'd planted it upside down.

At the end of the garden was a woodpile. Lady kept a sharp eye on it because she knew it was a place where rats liked to hide. As she came closer she spied a rat glaring at her from beneath the woodpile.

Barking, Lady leapt towards it. The rat was cornered. He came out on his hind feet ready to fight. When Lady growled and showed her sharp teeth, the rat scampered back under the woodpile. Lady dashed around the shed to catch him on the other side but she was too late. The rat had disappeared through a hole in the fence. Lady dug madly at the hole but the sound of a bicycle bell made her pause.

The local newspaper boy came riding along the street, whistling a tune and tossing newspapers onto front porches. Lady dashed for her front yard and was just in time to catch the paper.

Lady carried the paper up the stairs to

her private swinging door. But the newspaper was too wide for the door. Finally as Lady jumped in, there was a loud tearing sound.

Inside, Jim Dear and Darling were having breakfast. Lady placed the paper at Jim Dear's feet. "Clever girl," he said as he sipped his coffee. He reached for the paper, opened it up and sighed, "Look...she's done it again."

Darling burst out laughing. "Never mind,

Jim Dear. She tries to please and she is so adorable."

Darling looked admiringly at her pet. "Jim, she's grown into such a beautiful dog. She is an aristocrat...a true Lady."

Jim Dear nodded. "Say, she must be six months old by now. It's time we got her a dog license."

"Heavens, yes. And a collar, too."

Two days later, Darling walked into the livingroom and called Lady. Eagerly, she bounded in from the kitchen. "Look, Lady,

I've got a present for you," said Darling as she opened a package and lifted out a blue leather collar, studded with tiny gems.

"Do you like it?" She held the collar out towards Lady. Lady had seen some of her doggie friends wearing collars, but not as nice as this one. "Hope it fits," said Darling as she fastened the collar around Lady's neck. Darling took a small mirror from the wall and held it in front of Lady. "See how nice it looks. And so grown up. Jock and Trusty will be surprised when they see you today. Go along, show your scottie friend what a grand Lady you are now."

With a happy 'woof' Lady rushed off to visit Jock, the dog next door.

Jock was busy burying a bone in his secret hiding place when he heard Lady calling him. He quickly sat down on the hole so Lady would not see his collection of bones.

"Ah, there you are, Jock," said Lady. "Aren't you speaking to me today?"

"Oh, it's you, my bonnie lassie. I'll be with

you in a minute." He scraped some dirt over his hole.

"Notice anything different about me?" asked Lady, proud of her new collar.

"Oh, you've had a bath," said Jock.

"No..not that," said Lady impatiently. "I had one yesterday."

"Then you've had your nails clipped."

"No! No!" said Lady. "Guess again." She jingled her collar.

"Well...I guess I would'na be knowin then."

"Oh!" Lady looked very disappointed.

"Why, my bonnie lassie," he said sniffing the new leather, "It's a collar, a bonnie brand new collar. By the look of it, it must have been verra expensive!"

Lady tossed her head. "My folks are very good to me."

"Indeed they are. Have you shown it to Trusty yet?"

"No. You're my closest neighbor so I wanted you to know first," said Lady.

"Aye, lass. I appreciate that, but we'd best go to Trusty's at once. You know how sensitive he can be."

Together Lady and Jock trotted toward Trusty's house. They found him on the front porch fast asleep and dreaming.

"Trusty is probably dreaming about bygone days when he and his grandfather were trackin' criminals through the swamps," said Jock. "But that was before.."

"Before what?" asked Lady.

Jock looked sad. "'Tis time you knew the truth, lassie. It should'na happen to a dog, but well - Trusty has lost his sense of smell!"

Lady gasped. "Oh, no! How awful!"

"Aye, it is indeed. But we must never let on that we know."

Trusty, still sniffing, woke up. "Hi you two. Why, Miss Lady, you have a collar! And such a smart one, too. How time does fly."

"Aye," said Jock. "It seems like only yesterday she was cutting her teeth on Jim Dear's slippers and now...there she is a full-grown Lady. It's grand to be wearing the greatest honor a man can bestow."

"That's right, Miss Lady," said Trusty. "As my grandpappy, Ol' Reliable used to say...Don't recollect if I've ever mentioned Ol' Reliable before..."

"Aye, you have, laddie." Jock tried not to sound bored. He and Lady had both heard the tales of Trusty's grandpappy many times before.

"Oh," said Trusty,"I don't recollect having mentioned it, but I guess..."

There was the sound of a loud shrill whistle. Lady pricked up her ears. "It's Jim Dear. I must go. Please excuse me."

And with a bark she tore after Jim Dear who was walking along the street.

"Hello there, Lady. Come on, I'll beat you home!" said Jim Dear. Lady easily won the race and was waiting for Jim Dear when he reached the porch. "What have we here? A new collar. You're really grown up now."

Darling appeared at the door. "She's as adorable as ever. The nicest Christmas present I ever had. I can't imagine anything ever taking her place in our hearts."

Chapter Three

On the outskirts of the town lay the railroad tracks. Snooty people sometimes referred to the area as 'the wrong side of town' and avoided going there. For others, it was a friendly place. As far as Tramp was concerned, it was right for him.

Tramp was a mongrel, known among the dog community as being stubborn, brave, and defiant. Tramp knew his way around and could take care of himself. Although he belonged to no one in particular, in another way he belonged to many people. He had friends in places that mattered...mainly cafes and restaurants not far from the railway. He visited them all in turn but didn't settle down anywhere. That was the way he wanted to live.

Tramp strutted along with his head cocked. He was not a handsome dog, but there was something about him that other dogs, especially female dogs, liked.

"Let's see...where will it be for breakfast this morning?" he asked. "Aha, I think I'll try Tony's, I haven't been there in a week." He crossed the street and scratched on a Dutch door. He could hear a man singing inside. He scratched at the door again and suddenly the door opened.

"You want your breakfast? Here are some nice bones for you."

Tramp barked his thank you and trotted off to enjoy his breakfast. Just then he spotted the dog-catcher's wagon. The dog-catcher was nailing a sign onto a fence. It said, "Warning. Notice is hereby given that any unlicensed dog will be immediately impounded."

Tramp growled low in his throat. He should keep well out of sight...but on the other hand, two of his buddies were already in the wagon. Tramp ran across the street and jumped onto the back step of the dog-catcher's van. "Hey! Pssst!" he called. When the sad-looking bulldog looked up he immediately brightened.

"Look who's here, Peg! It's da Tramp!"

"Hi ya, handsome" said Peg, a dog with long silky hair. She wagged her tail. "Come to join the party?" she asked.

"All right, all right, you two. Cut the wisecracks. There isn't time. I'll try to get you out." After a few tries, he managed to unlatch the door. "Quick! Move!" he said. But the dogcatcher had already spotted him.

"Hey! What the heck's going on?" yelled the dogcatcher in an angry voice. But Tramp was ready and nipped him on the leg. The man yelled. "You mangy mutt! Let go of me! I'll get you for this!" When the others had made their getaway Tramp dashed across the street and jumped over a wall. The dogcatcher chased him but he was no match for Tramp. "Come back here!" yelled the dogcatcher shaking his fist. Tramp grinned from his hiding place. He waited until the coast was clear, then stepped out. "This neighborhood won't be safe for me for a while," thought Tramp. "I think I'll visit the other side of town."

Meanwhile, back at Lady's house, something strange was going on. Jock and Trusty were worried when they saw how gloomy and sad their friend was.

"Darling won't take me for walks anymore, Jim called me 'that dog,'" said Lady, a tear sliding down her furry nose.

To Lady's surprise, Jock's shaggy black face broke into a grin. "Ha! Ha! Now dinna take it too seriously, lassie. After all, at a time like this.."

"Yes," cut in Trusty. "You see, Miss Lady, there comes a time in the lives of all humans when...the stork...you understand."

"What he's trying to say, Lady," said Jock, "is that Darling is expecting a wee bairn."

"He means a baby," explained Trusty.

Just then Tramp came trotting past Lady's yard. Peeking around the gate post he sat watching Lady and listening to the interesting conversation.

Jock went on talking to Lady.

"Babies...they resemble humans."

"But a mite smaller," added Trusty.

"Aye! And they walk on all fours," said Jock.

"And if I remember correctly," said Trusty, "they beller a lot."

"Aye! And they're verra expensive. You'll not be permitted to play wi' it," said Jock sadly.

"But," murmured Trusty, "they're awfully sweet."

This talk was too much for Tramp. He decided to join in so he strolled over to the three dogs. "Just a cute little bundle of..ah..trouble!" said Tramp.

Lady turned her head and stared at the stranger. He continued, "Yeah, they scratch, pinch, pull your ears...ah but shucks, any dog can take that. It's what they do to your happy home..." he said.

Pushing Jock aside, Tramp squeezed in next to Lady.

"Look here, laddie, who are you to barge in and..." Jock's voice shook with anger at the nerve of the strange dog.

"The voice of experience," answered Tramp. "Just wait 'til junior gets here. You get the urge for a nice, comfortable scratch and...'Put that dog out' they yell. Start barking at some strange mutt, it's 'Stop that racket, you'll wake the baby.' That nice warm bed by the fire? A leaky doghouse."

"Oh dear...oh dear..." Lady looked upset.

Jock jumped to his feet. "Dinna listen, lassie. No human is that cruel."

Trusty moved closer. "Miss Lady, every-body knows a dog's best friend is his human!"

"Oh come on fellas. You haven't fallen for that old line, have you?"

Jock was furious. "Off with ye! Off with ye!"

"Okay, okay." Tramp wasn't looking for a fight. He walked back to Lady's side. "But remember, Pigeon. A human heart has only so much room for love and affection. When a baby moves in, the dog moves out."

This was too much for Lady. She burst into tears.

Chapter Four

One day in the month of April, Darling, pale and unwell, phoned Jim Dear who was at work. He rushed home and a little while later the doctor arrived. It wasn't long before Lady heard a thin wail coming from the bedroom. "It's a boy!" cried Jim Dear. Creeping up the stairs, Lady peered into the bedroom and saw Darling propped up in bed holding a tiny human pup in her arms and singing him a lullaby.

All went well for six months until the day Darling and Jim Dear went away and Aunt Sarah came to stay with the baby. Aunt Sarah did not like dogs. She preferred cats and especially her two beautiful Siamese cats which she brought with her in a basket. When Aunt Sarah was busy with the baby, the two cats tore into the

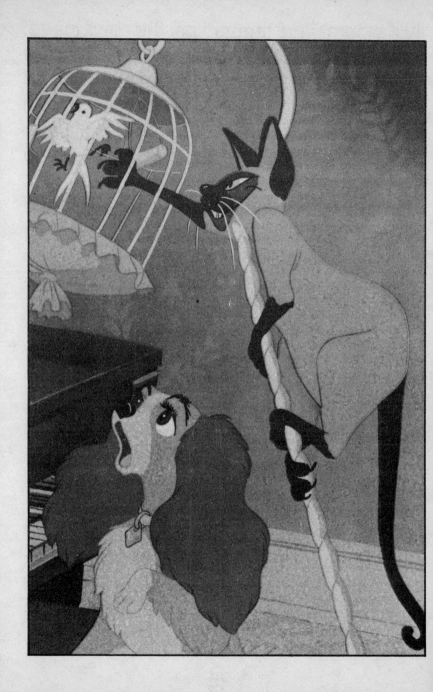

livingroom and leaped on the bird cage. The bird fluttered in terror. Quick as a flash, Lady charged at the cat. Licking their lips, the cats slyly jumped onto the sofa. Their faces seemed to say, "Later will do" and Lady knew the bird was in danger.

By now Lady was alarmed. "Oh," she thought, "if only Jim Dear and Darling would come back." But by now they were far away. Lady knew it was up to her to protect all property from the two cats.

There was a wail from the baby's room. Both cats stood still, listening. "Do you hear what I hear?" meowed one of them.

The other purred. "A baby cry. Where we find baby, there is milk nearby. There could be, plenty milk for you and also some for me!" The cats padded on velvety paws toward the stairs.

A warning bell sounded in Lady's head. The baby...the cats were going to attack the baby. They must be stopped at all costs. She flung herself between the cats and the stairs. Baring her sharp teeth she growled at the cats. They had the good sense to know that Lady meant business. They ran back into the livingroom with Lady hot on their heels. Springing to the window-sill, they clawed at the curtains until the curtains fell right on top of Lady

"Whatever is going on down there?" called Aunt Sarah.

"That's done it," said one of the cats. "Quick, put on an innocent face." The two cats huddled together, putting on an act of being scared. Lady had just freed herself from the fallen curtains when Aunt Sarah walked in the room.

"Merciful heavens!" she shrieked. "My darlings, my precious pets! Oh, you wicked animal." She glared at Lady.

Scooping up the two cats in her arms, she stomped toward the stairs. "I will take you both to my bedroom for safety until I have dealt with that beast!"

Lady was miserable. She had been sadly misjudged. But the worst was yet to come. Aunt Sarah returned to the livingroom. Her face was grim. She attached a

leash to Lady's collar and dragged her to a trolley. "To the pet shop," Aunt Sarah snarled to the conductor. When the trolley stopped Aunt Sarah got off, dragging Lady behind her. The pet shop smelled of straw and dog biscuits, the puppies yapped and the kittens meowed. Lady wished she were at home. Aunt Sarah was talking to the clerk.

"I want a muzzle...a good strong muzzle."

"Ah yes, ma'am. Now here's our latest combination leash and muzzle." He lifted

Lady onto the counter. "Now we'll just slip it on...no...no!" Lady was so frightened she tried to struggle free. Leaping off the counter, her leash caught in a birdcage which came crashing down. Lady was panic-stricken. She ran between Aunt Sarah's legs and straight out the door of the pet shop. Aunt Sarah screamed, "Lady, come back here...you come back here!"

Lady, still wearing the muzzle and leash, dodged in and out of traffic. She didn't pay attention to what direction she was going. She just ran and ran until her heart was pounding and she felt that she couldn't take another step.

Suddenly Lady saw Tramp! "Hey, Pigeon...what are you doing on this side of town? I thought you..." he broke off talking when he saw the muzzle. "Aw...you poor kid. We gotta get this off. And I think I know how."

Together they sneaked into the zoo and tricked a beaver into biting through the leather and freeing Lady. Lady, able to speak now, told Tramp about the terrible

things that had happened to her that day.

"Aunts...cats...muzzles, disgusting!" said Tramp. "That's what happens then you tie yourself down to one family."

"Haven't you got a family?" asked Lady.

"One for every day of the week," replied Tramp. "The point is, Pigeon, they don't have me!" Tramp told her about the restaurants he visited regularly. "Come **on**, I'll take you to Tony's."

Tony was glad to see Tramp and to meet his new friend, Lady. He served them a candlelit spaghetti dinner. Afterwards the two dogs took a stroll under the stars to the park. It was a romantic evening. Tramp gently licked Lady's face, then they quietly padded to a hill overlooking the park and settled down for the night.

Chapter Five

Lady awoke next morning with a start. "I should have been home hours ago," she said.

"Why?" said Tramp. "Who needs a home when you can live a life of excitement and adventure with me. Don't go back to life on a leash. Stay with me."

"But who would watch over the baby?" asked Lady.

Tramp knew when he was beaten. "Okay," he said with a sigh. "C'mon I'll take you home."

On the way to Lady's neighborhood they passed a chicken run. "Ever chase chickens, Pidge?" asked Tramp looking for some fun.

"Oh, we shouldn't," said Lady. But Tramp

was already crawling under the fence. She followed him and the two caused such a commotion that a man came out of the house with a gun and shot at them. While they were running away, Tramp jumped a high fence; but Lady was too tired. She slipped through some loose slats in the fence and right into the dogcatcher's net!

The net closed over Lady, pulling her up with a jerk. Gasping, she tried to fight her way out of the heavy mesh, but it was no use. Instead she was lifted up and thrown into the dogcatcher's wagon. "Might as well take this one straight to the Pound," said the dogcatcher gruffly.

"Pidge, Pidge! Where are you?" called Tramp. "I thought she was right behind me."

While Tramp searched for the missing Lady, she was on her way to the Dog Pound.

Arriving trembling and frightened she was led toward a cage. "Put her in number four, Bill," called a guard, "while I check her license number." The cell door was opened, Lady given a push, and the door slammed shut behind her.

Lady found herself in a cage with some rough-looking dogs. Toughy looked her over, a wide grin on his face. "Now look what we have here. Miss Park Avenoo, herself." Toughy and a bulldog moved in closer.

Toughy eyed Lady's collar and license. "And get a load of the crown jools she's wearin'." And he burst into nasty laughter.

Lady shrunk back into the corner as the two dogs moved closer. But help was at hand. The hubbub had awakened another dog called Peg. She jumped up and stood between Lady and the two dogs. "Lay off, will ya? Can't cha' see the poor kid's scared enough already?" Turning to Lady she said,"They don't mean no real harm. It's just your license."

Lady looked puzzled. "My license, what's the matter with my license?" she asked.

"There ain't nothing wrong with it, Dearie," said Peg. "It's just that it is your passport to freedom. Without it..."

She was interrupted by Toughy. "Hey, you guys," he whispered. "They're taking Nutsy on his last walk." The dogs crowded together at the bars as Nutsy, a sad-looking dog, was led past on a rope.

"Where is the guard taking him?" asked Lady.

"Through the one-way door, sister," answered Toughy.

"You mean...he's..." Lady was shattered.

"Oh, well, a short life and a merry one," said Bull.

Toughy scratched his back against the bars. "That's what the Tramp always says."

Lady pricked up her ears, looking surprised. "The Tramp?"

Toughy laughed. "He's given da slip to every dogcatcher in dis town."

"Ah, but remember my friends," added a wolfhound named Boris. "Tramp has his weaknesses, too."

Toughy and Bull winked at each other. "You mean the dames," Toughy said laughing. "He never takes 'em serious."

"Ah, but some day," said Boris, "he is

meeting someone deeferent. Someone delicate who is geeving him a wish to shelter and protect."

Bull interrupted. "Someone like Miss Park Avenoo, huh?" he said motioning to Lady.

Peg flipped her long hair from her eyes. "And under the spell of true love..."

"The poor chump gets careless..." added Bull.

"And he gets picked up," chimed in Toughy. "Then it's curtains for the Tramp."

Lady trembled. "Oh, no!" she thought. "Tramp mustn't grow careless - ever!"

The guard entered. "It's the little cocker, Bill, in number four." The guard reached inside the cage for Lady. "It's okay, baby, they've come to take you home."

Lady could hardly believe her ears. Jim Dear and Darling must have returned. Everything was going to be fine, after all. She waved goodbye to her new friends and headed for the door to freedom.

Chapter Six

When Lady left the Pound she had her first big disappointment. She was handed over to Aunt Sarah. Lady tried to thank Aunt Sarah for rescuing her, but all Aunt Sarah would say was 'Down, dog, down!' Lady crept into a corner of the cab until they reached home. Then with a happy bark she scampered up the pavement to the front door.

"Not that way, my girl," said Aunt Sarah sternly. "I have a special place for you."

Lady followed Aunt Sarah to the end of the garden. There stood a kennel. "You can stay in the doghouse," said Aunt Sarah. "Go along...in you go." Lady sadly started in the door when Aunt Sarah grabbed her collar and clipped a long chain to it.

"That will make sure you keep clear of the house," she snapped. Lady lay down on the wooden floor, sadder than she had ever been in her life.

A few weeks passed, with Lady still chained to the doghouse. She was feeling so unhappy that she didn't care about anything anymore. One gray morning when Lady was especially blue, Jock and Trusty came to visit. They were very worried about Lady after her terrible experience.

The two friends approached the kennel. Lady was not in sight. "Lassie!" called Jock.

"Miss Lady, ma'am," joined in Trusty. Lady lay inside her doghouse her head resting on her velvety paws. She didn't look up. "Please, I don't want to see anybody."

"Lassie, we have a way to help you."

"Aye!" joined in Jock. "We both have very comfortable homes..."

"That's right," continued Trusty. "Where we know you'll be welcome and appreciated, Miss Lady."

Lady shook her head. "You're both very kind, but..." She broke off in mid-sentence. Rushing towards them was Tramp, a juicy bone in his mouth.

"Oh, Pigeon!" he said. "Oh, Pidge!"

Jock and Trusty glared at him and Lady tossed her head. All three dogs turned their backs on Tramp. Tramp moved towards Lady and dropped the juicy bone behind her. "Little something I picked up for you, Pidge!"

Lady glanced at the bone then walked

away, nose in the air. She was pulled up short by the chain attached to her doghouse. Trying to look dignified, she sat down. Tramp walked around to the front of the doghouse. "Looks like I'm the one in the doghouse," he said.

Trusty rose to leave. Jock followed him and then turned to face Tramp. "You...you mongr-r-rel," he growled. Then both dogs left the yard.

Tramp was wretched and forlorn. Not only had he been snubbed and put in his place but now Lady wouldn't speak to him.

Noticing the bone Tramp had dropped, she kicked it across the yard. "Goodbye!" she cried. "And take this with you!" Then she disappeared inside her doghouse.

The gray sky grew darker than ever as if a storm was about to spring up. Tramp stood at the kennel door but Lady would not see him or speak to him. With heavy steps but a heavier heart, Tramp walked to a loose board in the fence. Inside the doghouse Lady cried until her cheeks and paws were wet. She loved Tramp but she was sending him away because he was a rascal, a no-good.

Before Tramp stepped through the fence, he looked back to see if there was any sign that Lady would forgive him. But the kennel door was shut.

Inside Lady was listening for the sound of Tramp leaving. When she heard the fence board slam back into place she lay down by the door. Tears still shone in her eyes and she was very, very sad.

Suddenly the storm broke and a bright flash of lightning lit up the street for a second. Among the bushes in the neighboring yard a pair of mean bright eyes peered out. A large gray rat scurried across the street, through a hole in Lady's fence, and dashed towards Jim Dear's woodpile.

Lady, too unhappy to bother about the storm, suddenly opened her eyes wide as she saw the rat. She stood up, her coat bristling, and growled. Rats spelled danger...she must drive it from the garden. Lady barked and barked.

Surely Aunt Sarah would realize that there was something wrong.

The rat, its coat shiny with rain, reached the roof. It stopped, then crawled along the gutter. Lady yelped and howled. The lightning lit up the sky and thunder roared and echoed like an angry giant. A light flashed in the upper window and the rat, scared by the light, scampered in the other direction.

Aunt Sarah raised the window, yelling loudly, "Stop that! Stop that at once!"

Lady crouched down, quiet for a moment. Then she saw the rat continue along the edge of the roof. She began barking again.

"Hush now! Hush!" Aunt Sarah tried to silence Lady but it was no use. Lady's eyes opened wide with horror. The unthinkable had happened. The nursery window was open at the bottom ...the rat had crawled into the baby's room! Oh, how to make Aunt Sarah understand! But she was not in the mood to listen. Instead she ordered Lady to be quiet. Poor Lady! She had done her best. It was her job to protect the baby, but she couldn't do anything chained to the doghouse.

Tramp appeared through the slat in the fence. "What's wrong, Pidge?"

"A rat," answered Lady. "Upstairs, in the baby's room."

"How'll I get in?" asked Tramp.

"The little door on the porch," said Lady, nodding toward the back porch where Jim Dear had fixed her private swinging door. Those happy days seemed so far away now.

Within seconds Tramp had gone through

the door and was inside the house. He looked around - he didn't want to run into Aunt Sarah before he'd had a chance to get the rat. Quietly he padded up the carpeted stairs. He moved on and when he reached the second door, he knew he had found the nursery. The door was partially open and there was the smell of milk and baby powder. Slowly he entered. The baby was taking a nap. A sudden flash of lightning showed the rat on the ground, close to the crib.

Tramp's hackles stood on end. Growling, he moved slowly toward the rat, guided by the evil glow from the rat's eyes. The rat moved to a chair never taking his eyes off Tramp. There was a short scuffle but the rat managed to get away. Tramp chased him around and around in the darkness.

The sly rat doubled back and crouched beneath the crib. When it found its way blocked, it darted in the other direction. But Tramp was too fast for it and they came face to face.Tramp rushed in, pawing at the rat and knocked it into the air. It landed on its four feet and then stood up on its hind legs. The rat knew it was fighting for its life and it fought with every vicious bone in its body.

In the yard Lady was pacing nervously. What was going on in the house? She gave a mighty tug on her chain. Lady was surprised when suddenly the chain broke and she was free. She ran to the porch door, the chain dragging behind her.

In the nursery the fight continued. The rat jumped onto the chair, then the dresser. The rat was hiding in the corner of the crib when Lady arrived at the nursery doorway. Tramp dived at the rat but missed and by accident knocked over the crib. Lady ran to the baby while Tramp chased the rat around the room. Furniture went flying to all corners of the room. It looked like a disaster area.

Aunt Sarah was resting. She didn't like storms but now she sat up in bed. She had heard something. Her ears had picked up the sound of a thin wail. "The baby must be awake and need me," she thought as she hurried toward the nursery.

Tramp, never a dog to give up, tried to trap the rat. When he dove at the rat he became tangled in the curtains and they fell on top of him. The baby stopped crying and shook his rattle. Lady licked his little hands as Tramp limped over to the two of them. Lady looked at Tramp, her hero. He had saved the day...and certainly saved the baby.

A moment later Aunt Sarah appeared in the doorway. She gasped as she looked around the room at the terrible mess then rushed forward and grabbed up the baby. Lady and Tramp smiled at each other. This was their special moment.

"Oh, merciful heavens, you poor darling. Thank goodness you're not hurt," said Aunt Sarah hugging the baby. She righted the crib and placed the baby safely inside. Then she turned to Lady and Tramp. "You vicious brutes!" she yelled. Grabbing a broom from the closet, she swished it at Tramp saying, "Back! Get back!" until she had backed him into the closet and closed the door on him. "Now," said Aunt Sarah. "The Pound! That's it, I'll call the Pound."

Those words fell on Lady's ears like the crack of doom. Her darling Tramp, the hero, locked up in the Pound. She barked angrily but Aunt Sarah stepped on her chain, picked it up and dragged her downstairs. Lady howled and pulled but it was no use. Aunt Sarah couldn't have cared less about dogs. "Come on! I'll call them this minute. I couldn't rest with that brute in the house."

An hour passed, maybe longer. Lady,locked in the cellar, had lost track of time. Outside the thunderstorm had blown over. A streetcar pulled up and two familiar figures stepped down. Jim Dear and Darling had come home.

"Darling, look! The Pound wagon," said Jim Dear. "What's going on?"

Jim Dear and Darling broke into a run, passing Jock and Trusty who were hiding behind some bushes, watching events.

"Say, what's going on here?" called Jim Dear to the dogcatcher.

"Just pickin' up a stray, mister. C'mon giddap! Caught him attackin' a baby!"

"My baby!" shrieked Darling, dashing up the front walk. "Aunt Sarah! Aunt Sarah!" Jim Dear and Darling disappeared into the house.

Lady was still lying in the dark cellar. Hearing voices, she scratched at the door and waited but no one heard her. Aunt Sarah was speaking. "Thank goodness I got there in time. There they were, crib overturned..."

Jim Dear sounded puzzled. "There must be some mistake. I know Lady wouldn't..."

Lady began barking as loud as she could. Jim Dear was home! He opened the cellar door and she rushed toward him, licking his hands and face in welcome. Then she dashed to the foot of the stairs. She had to make him understand - and there was so little time. "Oh!" shrieked Aunt Sarah. "That dog's loose! Keep her away!"

"Nonsense!" replied Jim Dear. "She's

trying to tell us something." Lady dashed up the stairs."What is it, girl?" He followed Lady into the nursery.

Lady ran to the fallen curtains. "Lady," asked Jim Dear. "What are you trying..."

Bending forward he lifted the curtains and there lay the dead rat. Now he knew what Lady had wanted to tell him. "Darling...Aunt Sarah! Come here!" yelled Jim Dear.

The two women hurried to the nursery. "What is it, Jim Dear?" asked Darling. Aunt Sarah peered over his shoulder. "Ah! Ah! A rat!" she cried in horror.

Jim Dear stroked Lady's head. "And Lady knew all the time. Clever girl. Thank heavens that she did."

Trusty and Jock had been standing in the shadows of the porch, watching and listening. When they heard Aunt Sarah screech,"A rat!" they looked at each other.

So poor Tramp was innocent. He had been trying to save the baby...not attack it. And now he was on his way to be destroyed.

"A rat!" said Trusty. "We should have known."

Jock shook his head sadly. "I misjudged him - badly."

Trusty suddenly rushed down the porch steps. "C'mon. We got to stop the wagon!"

"But we dinna know which way they've gone!" said Jock.

"The scent! Follow the scent!"

"Uh, let's face it, mon." said Jock. "We both know you've lost your sense of smell." Nose to nose the two dogs faced each other and Trusty gave a snort. He continued sniffing the ground. He had to show Jock that he was wrong. At last he picked up the scent. Baying loudly, he ran off down the street leaving Jock far behind. Jock followed as fast as his little legs could carry him.

Trusty ran through the water, searching for the scent. Then he flung back his head and bayed. Jock knew things were going in their favor. Then all of a sudden, there it was ahead of them...the Pound wagon.

With a burst of energy, the dogs raced

after the wagon, barking loudly.

Inside Tramp, who was sure this was his last ride, perked up. Was it possible...just possible that he might be rescued? The wagon bounced on a rough section of roadway while Jock and Trusty ran along by the wheel. Trusty leapt ahead trying to stop the horses, baying as loudly as any bloodhound has ever done.

Hearing all the commotion, the dogcatcher looked down and saw the two dogs. "Go on!" he yelled. "Get out of here."

The horses began to move faster. "Easy boys," the driver yelled to them. "Whoa...whoa." But the frightened horses galloped on. Trusty's loud baying and Jock's barking scared the horses so that they reared up, their hooves pawing the air. The dogcatcher tried to stop them. "Watch it! Watch it!" he called but it was too late. The wagon swerved, then with a wild lurch, tipped over onto its side.

Trusty was not fast enough to move out of the way. As the wagon hit the ground, his body struck the bars of the wagon. His heroic efforts to stop the Pound wagon had been successful - but he had paid a high price. Unmoving, he lay stretched out on the wet ground.

Back at Lady's house, Jim Dear had been thinking how grateful he was to Lady, but also to Tramp for saving the baby. He knew that at that very moment the luckless dog was being carted off to his doom. Without wasting time on explanations to Darling or Aunt Sarah, but scooping Lady into his arms, he dashed to the street and hailed a passing cab. A little later the cab slowed down as they came upon the place in the road where the wagon had overturned. A crowd had gathered around the wagon trying to calm the skittish horses.

Tramp, unharmed by the crash, was standing at the bars staring out. Lady spotted Tramp and gave a short, sharp bark. When the cab stopped she jumped out and raced across to Tramp. "Hi, Pidge," he said softly. "It's sure good to see you!" Lady held her head sideways and Tramp lovingly licked her cheek. Lady was so happy. From now on, Jim Dear would take care of everything.

But her moment of happiness didn't last long. A painful whining made her look around. Not far away, Jock, mud-spattered and miserable, was standing beside Trusty. The bloodhound lay under the wagon wheel, his eyes shut tight, his body still. Lady jumped down from the wagon and ran towards them. Jock tried to rouse his pal, but there was no sign of life.

Chapter Seven

Several weeks had passed since the night of Tramp's rescue. It was now Christmas Eve and the town lay silent beneath a blanket of snow. Inside Jim Dear and Darling's house, Jim Dear was trying to line up the family for a photograph. But it wasn't easy. Lady's puppies wouldn't cooperate! Three of the puppies looked just like Lady, but one was an exact replica of Tramp, his father. Jim Dear and Darling had insisted on adopting Tramp and he now stood proudly wearing his new leather collar and license.

The front gate opened. "Darling," called Jim Dear. "We have visitors."

"Visitors?" Darling ran to the window, Tramp at her heels.

Jock was standing at the front gate waiting for someone. Then Trusty, walking very slowly stepped into view.

"Why, it's Jock," cried Darling.

"And good old Trusty." Jim Dear leaned further out the window watching the two friends make their way up the path.

Trusty's foot was bandaged and in a splint so he was forced to walk slowly and carefully on the icy ground.

Tramp was jumping up and down with excitement. Trusty and Jock were now his good friends. "All right, boy - all right," said Jim Dear, petting Tramp's head. "We'll let 'em in." Jim Dear opened the street door. "Well, Merry Christmas," he greeted the two callers. "Come in.. come in. I'll see about refreshments." He called up the stairs, "Darling, where did you put the dog biscuits? You know, the box Aunt Sarah sent for Christmas?"

Lady and Tramp stood happily side by side, looking proudly at their family. "Well," said Jock talking to Tramp, "I see you finally have a collar."

Trusty moved forward. "Oh, yeah. A new collar. I caught the scent the moment I came into the house." He sat down. "Trusty, ah says to myself, somebody is wearin' a new collar. 'Course, my sense of smell is very highly developed. Runs in the family, ya know."

Trusty grinned and the four puppies lined up in front of him as he began his familiar story. "As mah grandpappy, Ol' Reliable used to say,er,don't recollect if ah've ever mentioned Ol' Reliable before."

"No, you haven't Uncle Trusty," piped up two of the puppies in unison.

"Huh - ah haven't? Well, as Ol' Reliable used to say - he'd say..ah..ah...he'd say ...er... You know ah...ah clean forgot what he used to say!"

Lady, Tramp, and Jock chuckled, and the puppies went back to their play, tugging on Trusty's ears and running round and round the Christmas tree. Outside the snow drifted lazily to earth. In the street carolers sang hymns of peace and goodwill while Christmas candles flickered softly in the windows. There could not have been a happier or more joyful Christmas Eve.